To Bentley

The RUMOR

A Jataka Tale from India

Retold & Illustrated by

Jan Thornhill

from Sonshine Children's Centre

MAPLE
TREE
PRESS

Maple Tree Press Inc.
51 Front Street East, Suite 200, Toronto, Ontario M5E 1B3
www.mapletreepress.com

Text and Illustrations © 2002 Jan Thornhill
First Paperback Edition, 2005

Distributed in Canada by Raincoast Books
9050 Shaughnessy Street, Vancouver, British Columbia V6P 6E5

Distributed in the United States by Publishers Group West
1700 Fourth Street, Berkeley, California 94710

We acknowledge the financial support of the Canada Council for the Arts,
the Ontario Arts Council, the Government of Canada through the Book Publishing
Industry Development Program (BPIDP), and the Government of Ontario through the
Ontario Media Development Corporation's Book Initiative for our publishing activities.

Cataloguing in Publication Data
Thornhill, Jan
The rumor : a Jataka tale from India / retold & illustrated by Jan
Thornhill. — 1st pbk. ed.

ISBN 1-897066-27-9
I. Title.

PS8589.H5497R84 2005   jC813'.54   C2004-904662-4

Design & art direction: Jan Thornhill
Illustrations: Jan Thornhill

Printed in China

A   B   C   D   E   F

Long, long ago, in India, a young hare lived in a sun-dappled grove of palm and mango trees. This hare was a worrywart. She worried about food, she worried about rain, she worried about her eyes being green. She worried and fretted about everything.

One day she curled up in her favorite spot in the shade to have a nap. Nap time was when the young hare did all her best worrying, and this time a scary thought occurred to her. "What if the world breaks up," she wondered. "What will happen to me?"

Just then, a ripe mango broke free from a branch and crashed down on a crunchy old palm frond behind the hare. It made such a loud sound she thought it was an explosion.

"OH, NO!" she cried. "The world *is* breaking up!"

Leaping to her feet, she ran through the palm and mango grove as fast as her hippity-hop legs could carry her. She was so frightened she didn't look back to see what had made the noise, not even once. She just ran.

The worrywart hare passed another hare who was nibbling on flowers. "Why are you running?" he called out to her.

Without slowing down, she answered, "The world is breaking up! Run for your life!"

"OH, NO!" cried the second hare, and took flight alongside her.

As they ran farther through the palm grove, one hare after another heard the rumor that the world was breaking up. One by one, they joined in the race to escape until there were a thousand hares all pattering along together.

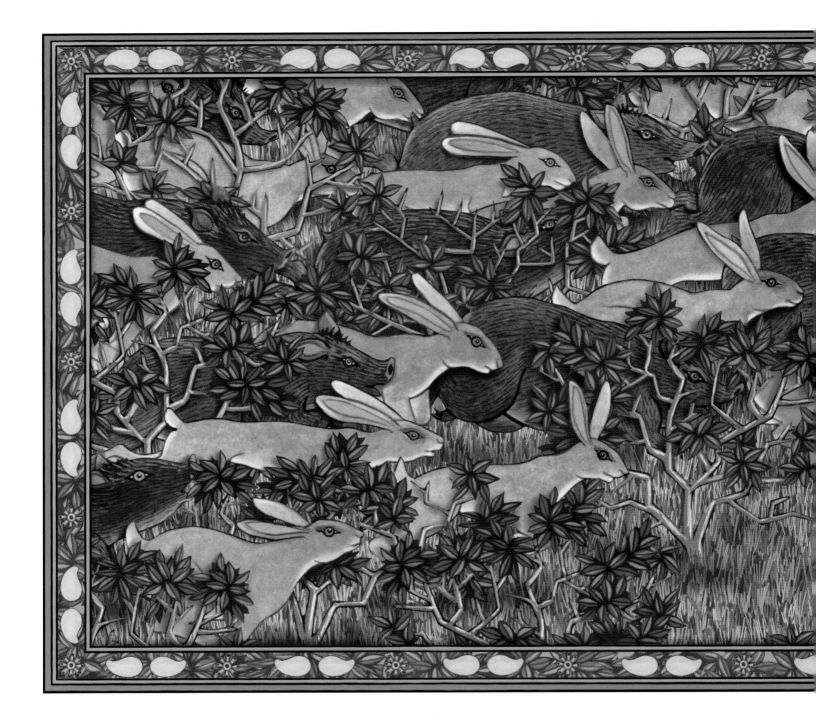

Eventually, the hares ran from the palm grove into the thicket, home of the boars. They passed a boar who was rooting in the soil with his snout. "Why are you running?" he shouted.

"The world is breaking up!" one of the hares answered. "Run for your life!"

"OH, NO!" grunted the boar, and took flight alongside the hares.

As the frightened animals ran, one boar after another heard the rumor and joined the crowd until there were a thousand boars and a thousand hares all crashing through the thicket together.

Eventually the hares and boars ran from the thicket into the marshland, home of the deer. They passed a deer browsing on tender leaves. "Why are you running?" she called out.

"The world is breaking up!" one of the boars answered. "Run for your life!"

"OH, NO!" cried the deer, and took flight alongside the hares and boars.

As the frightened animals ran, one deer after another heard the rumor and joined the crowd until there were a thousand deer, a thousand boars and a thousand hares all splashing across the marshland together.

Eventually the hares and boars and deer ran from the marshland into the forest, home of the tigers. They ran by a tiger basking in the sun. "Why are you running?" he shouted.

"The world is breaking up!" one of the deer answered. "Run for your life!"

"OH, NO!" bellowed the tiger, and took flight alongside the hares and boars and deer.

As the frightened animals ran, one tiger after another heard the rumor and joined the crowd until there were a thousand tigers, a thousand deer, a thousand boars and a thousand hares all pounding through the forest together.

Eventually the animals ran from the forest into the brushland, home of the rhinoceroses.

They ran past a rhinoceros tearing leaves off a shrub. "Why are you running?" she called out to them.

"The world is breaking up!" one of the tigers answered. "Run for your life!"

"OH, NO!" squeaked the rhinoceros, and took flight alongside the others.

As the frightened animals ran, one rhinoceros after another heard the rumor and joined the crowd until there were a thousand rhinoceroses, a thousand tigers, a thousand deer, a thousand boars and a thousand hares all thundering across the brushland.

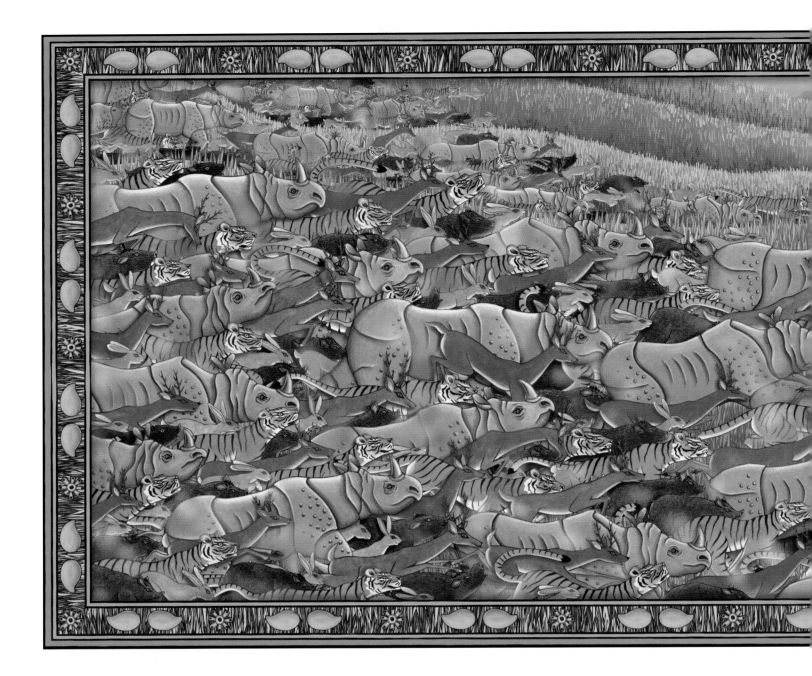

Eventually the huge stampede of animals ran from the brushland into the open plain, home of the lions. The great rumble interrupted a lion who'd been quietly grooming himself. "Why are you running?" he shouted when the animals were close enough to hear.

"The world is breaking up!" a rhinoceros answered. "Run for your life!"

Now this lion, although he was quite young, was nonetheless very wise. So, instead of joining the crowd without question, he looked far off beyond the end of the stampede for a sign that the world was, indeed, breaking up. He saw nothing. There were no explosions in the distance. There was no smoke, no fire.

The lion thought to himself: These animals are in such a panic, somebody's going to get hurt. So he ran to the head of the stampede, opened his giant mouth and roared his loudest roar.

As everyone knows, if there's one thing scarier than the world breaking up, it's the roar of a lion. So, naturally, all the animals dug in their hooves and paws and claws and skidded to a stop.

When the dust had settled and everyone had untangled themselves and it was completely quiet, the lion turned to the rhinoceroses.

"Who saw the world breaking up?" he asked.

"The tigers know all about it," said the rhinoceroses.

The lion asked the tigers.

The tigers shrugged and said, "Ask the deer."

The deer put the blame on the boars. The boars said they heard it from the hares.

The lion turned to the hares. "So," he said, "which one of you saw the world breaking up?"

"It was HER," the hares all cried out together, pointing to the young worrywart hare.

The lion faced the young hare. "Well?" he said, in his deep, rumbly lion voice.

Though the worrywart hare was quivering in fear, she told the lion she'd heard the world breaking up while she was napping in the palm and mango grove.

"And what did the world breaking up look like?" asked the lion.

"I don't really know," admitted the hare. "I was so scared, I just ran."

"Hmm," said the wise lion.

He turned to the rest of the animals. "All of you wait here," he commanded. "This hare and I will go and see if the world really is breaking up."

The lion put the worrywart hare on his back. "Hold on tight!"
he said. Then he raced like the wind, over the plain and brushland,

through the forest trees, across the marshland and thicket, not once stopping until they had arrived at the palm and mango grove.

"Show me where you were napping," said the lion.

The hare pointed to her favorite spot in the shade.

The lion padded over to have a look.

"Aha!" he said. There, lying on a crunchy old palm frond, was a freshly fallen mango. "You must have heard this mango fall, not the world breaking apart."

"Oh," said the hare in a tiny voice. She felt foolish.

The lion put her on his back again and off they raced to tell the others — through the palm grove and thicket, over the marshland, through the forest trees and brushland and out into the open plain where the thousand rhinoceroses, the thousand tigers, the thousand deer, the thousand boars, and the thousand hares were all waiting to hear the juicy details about the world breaking up.

"What a silly mistake!" said the lion. "Didn't any of you check
to see whether or not the world really *was* breaking up?"

The rhinoceroses looked at their toes and shuffled their feet.
The tigers cleaned their whiskers. The deer whistled silly tunes.
The boars nudged their snouts in the ground. The hares looked up

at the sky and hummed. Everybody was pretty embarrassed.

"The world's fine," the lion said kindly. "There's absolutely nothing to worry about. Go home, now, everyone."

And so they did. The thousand rhinoceroses returned to their home
in the brushland, the thousand tigers to theirs in the forest, the

thousand deer to the marshland, the thousand boars to the thicket, and the thousand hares to the palm and mango grove.

When the young worrywart hare got home, she was very tired. All that excitement and running and missing her nap had worn her right out. She was so tired that when she curled up in her favorite spot in the shade of the palm and mango trees she went right to sleep without worrying about anything at all.

The Rumor is a retelling of an ancient Jataka tale from India. Jataka tales have been used for more than 2,500 years to teach about sharing, compassion, and the difference between good and bad. In many Jataka tales, the Buddha appears as an animal. Can you guess which Indian animal he is in this story?

Hares have long ears and strong legs. They eat all kinds of greenery, but they like grasses the most. Unlike rabbits, which are born hairless and helpless, hares are completely covered in fur with their eyes open at birth, and can hop alongside their mother soon after. One of the rarest types is the Bristly Hare of India.

The smallest wild boar in the world is the Pygmy Hog of India. Pygmy hogs live in small family groups and feed mostly on roots they dig from the ground. They make nests to sleep in by digging a ditch with their hooves and snouts, then bending surrounding grasses over the top.

Swamp Deer live where they can feed on grasses and water plants. They sometimes bark like dogs when they are frightened, especially when predators, such as tigers, are near. They are able to threaten an attacker with their sharp antlers.

The tiger is the largest member of the cat family. Tigers have huge muscles and can jump almost the length of a house. They silently creep up on their prey on feet with very soft pads. When they hunt at night for deer, boars, and even young elephants, they can see five times better than people can.

The Indian Rhinoceros has a single horn on its snout and a hide as thick and tough as armor. Rhinoceroses make a number of different sounds including honks, squeaks, and grunts. They use their flexible upper lips to pull grasses, leaves, and water plants into their mouths. In the heat of the day, they like to wallow in the cool water of ponds and puddles.

The Asiatic Lion of India is much like the African lion, but is slightly smaller and has a shorter mane. Lions live in small family groups, called prides. They hunt together for deer and other hoofed animals. A female can have one to five cubs in a litter. The Asiatic lion once roamed as far west as Greece, but today can only be found wild in a single forest in India.

Although large numbers of these animals are shown in **The Rumor***, it would be impossible to see so many today. All these species — Bristly Hare, Pygmy Boar, Swamp Deer, Bengal Tiger, Indian Rhinoceros, and Asiatic Lion — are either endangered or threatened, mostly because of loss of habitat.*

The Rumor is based on "The Timid Hare and the Flight of the Beasts" from *The Jataka; or, Stories of the Buddha's Former Births*, edited by E. B. Cowell (Cambridge University Press, 1897).